A TEAM STAYS TOGETHER!

by Tony and Lauren Dungy

illustrated by
Vanessa Brantley Newton

Ready-to-Read

Simon Spotlight
New York   London   Toronto   Sydney   New Delhi

SIMON SPOTLIGHT
An imprint of Simon & Schuster Children's Publishing Division
1230 Avenue of the Americas, New York, New York 10020
Text copyright © 2011 by Tony Dungy and Lauren Dungy
Illustrations copyright © 2011 by Vanessa Brantley Newton
All rights reserved, including the right of reproduction in whole or in part in any form.
SIMON SPOTLIGHT, READY-TO-READ, and colophon are registered trademarks of
Simon & Schuster, Inc.
For information about special discounts for bulk purchases, please contact Simon & Schuster
Special Sales at 1-866-506-1949 or business@simonandschuster.com.
Manufactured in the United States of America 0112 LAK
10 9 8 7 6 5 4 3
Cataloging-in-Publication Data for this book is available from the Libary of Congress.
ISBN 978-1-4424-3539-1 (pbk)
ISBN 978-1-4424-3540-7 (hc)
ISBN 978-1-4424-3541-4 (eBook)

Today was the big game.
The whole Dungy family
was clapping and shouting.
Jade and Jordan were waving
at their big brother, Eric.
Justin was waving at the duck.

"Yay, team!" They all cheered.
Mom and Dad yelled,
"Touchdown!"
Everyone was having
fun at the game.

"Peanuts! Popcorn! Pretzels!"
shouted the man selling treats.
Justin heard his tummy rumble.

"I'm hungry, Mom," said Justin.

"I'm starving, Dad," said Jordan.

"I'm both!" said Jade.

"Let's wait a few minutes," Dad said.

"It's almost halftime."

"Yes, we'll go soon," said Mom.

"Okay," said Justin and Jade.
"Okay," said Jordan, "but I'm
still starving."
Just then Dad stood up and said,
"It's halftime. Let's go."
Everyone jumped up and shouted,
"Hooray!"

"Hang on," Mom said. "It's really crowded. Let's all stay together." Dad agreed. "Everybody stay together," he said.

"I want cotton candy," said Justin.
"I want popcorn," said Jade.
"I want a hot dog," said Jordan.
"And hats, too!" the kids said
together.

There were all kinds of yummy
food places. Everything smelled
so good! And everyone kept
changing their minds.
Justin got a pretzel
instead of cotton candy.
Jade got ice cream
instead of popcorn.

What did Jordan want?

Wait.

"Where is Jordan?" Jade asked.

"Oh no!" said Mom.

Mom and Dad looked upset.

"Let's go back to where we were," said Dad.
"Jordan!" called Justin.
They looked at the ice-cream stand.

No Jordan.

"Jordan!" called Jade.
They looked at the popcorn stand.
No Jordan.

"Jordan!" called Mom.
They looked at the pretzel stand.
No Jordan.

"Jordan!" called Dad.
They looked at
the cotton-candy stand.
They even looked at
the T-shirt store.
No Jordan anywhere.

Justin saw a security guard.
"Sir, have you seen my brother?"
he asked.
"What does he look like?"
the man asked.

"He looks just like me,"
Justin said.
"And he's wearing a green and
yellow shirt."
Where could Jordan be?

Justin and Jade could tell
that Mom and Dad were getting
worried.
"He wanted a hot dog," said Jade.
"We need to look there."

"Let's split up," said Mom.
Mom took Justin to the
hot-dog stand.
Dad took Jade back to
the T-shirt store.

Dad and Jade didn't see him.
"We'll find him, Dad," said Jade.
Now she was getting worried too.
"We sure will," said Dad.

Mom and Justin turned the corner.
Dad and Jade turned the corner.
And there was Jordan looking
at the hat stand.

Mom and Dad ran up to him.
Jade and Justin hugged
their brother.

"I can't believe you lost me!"
Jordan said.
"We have been everywhere
looking for you!"
Justin told his brother.
"I was right here looking at
these hats," Jordan said.

Jordan pointed to the silliest thing
the kids had ever seen.
It was a quacking-duck hat.

When Jordan squeezed the duck bill,
the hat quacked and
the tail feathers wiggled!
Everybody giggled.
"But now," Jordan announced,
"all I want to see is a big box
of popcorn!"

"And all I want to see is you,"
Mom said. "Please stay close by
this time."
"Yes, let's stay together," Dad said.
"We are a team. And a team
stays together!"

"Okay, Jordan," Mom said.
"Where do they sell the popcorn?"
Justin ran ahead and said,
"This way! I saw popcorn
at the hot dog place, and now
I'm hungry again!"

"Me too!" said Jade. "Let's go."
Jordan turned to his little brother
and sister and said, "You guys need
to stay where Mom can see you.
Remember, we are a team.
And a team stays together!"
Mom looked at Dad.
Justin looked at Jade.

Jordan had a funny smile
on his face.

"Now where have I heard that before?" Dad said. "That's a good thing to remember, Jordan. Even if you see hats that wiggle and quack. So come on, team, let's go!"

Off the family went
to get popcorn for Jordan
and to watch more football.
Together.